This Book
Belongs to

Eva

For Rowan and Ruis – M. R.

For Caroline, the best agent in the world! – T. McL.

PUFFIN BOOKS

UK | USA | Canada | Ireland | Australia | India | New Zealand | South Africa
Puffin Books is part of the Penguin Random House group of companies
whose addresses can be found at global.penguinrandomhouse.com.

www.penguin.co.uk   www.puffin.co.uk   www.ladybird.co.uk

 Penguin
Random House
UK

First published 2017
001

 MIX
Paper from
responsible sources
FSC® C018179

Michelle Robinson & Tom McLaughlin

CHICKEN NUGGET
IN SCRAMBLED
EGG

PUFFIN

Burger
(My big brother)

Mama

Fillet
& Drumstick
(the twins)

My name is Nugget,
Chicken Nugget.
This is my family.
I'm the smallest . . .
But not for much longer.

Benedict

My baby brother, Benedict, will be hatching soon.

"Stupid babies," says my big brother Burger.

"Yeah," says my other brother Drumstick.

"Babies are boring."

"Shh," Mama says. "It's not nice to pick on people who are smaller than you. Besides, Benedict can hear EVERY word."

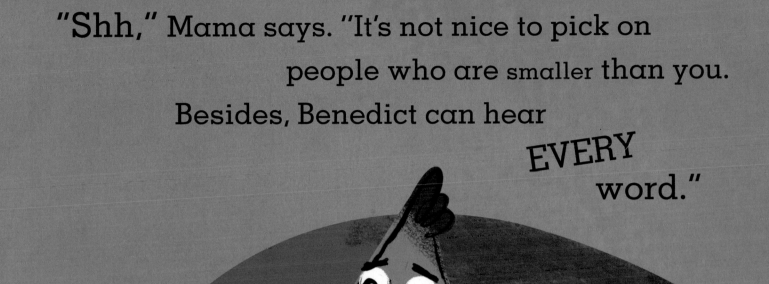

Knit an egg cosy

I'll NEVER pick on Benedict.
I'm going to be kind to my little brother.

See? I even let him share my crayons.

I think he looks much better,
but Mama doesn't agree.

"Oh, Nugget," she sighs.
"Why don't you take
Benedict outside to play?
Take extra-special
care of him – and
wrap up warm."

It's cold outside,
        but I'm keeping warm by kicking the ball.
So I let Benedict borrow my cart.
            He's cosy,
        I'm having fun
                – everybody's happy.

I'm so kind that I even let Benedict join in.

"KICK!"

I yell.

But if he *can* hear every word he clearly isn't listening.

That's when Fillet and Drumstick
come and spoil everything.

"Boring Benedict,"
            says Fillet.

"Yeah," says Drumstick.
            "Benedict can't kick. He can't even run."

"Shh," I say. "He can hear EVERY word!"
But they don't care.

"You babies are so boring,"
            says Fillet. "Let's go."

And they leave me on my own with Benedict.
I give up. What's the point of being kind
if you're still smaller than everybody else?

That's when our neighbour, Mrs Kiev,
pops her head over the fence.

"Baby blues, dearie?" she says huskily.

"Why, Mrs Kiev," I say,
"what furry arms you have today."

"All the better to warm you with," she coos at Benedict.
"Why don't you let me look after the baby while you play?"

"I'm supposed to be taking care of him,"
I say. "He's only little."

"Small and sweet," says Mrs Kiev,
licking her lips. "Now you deserve
a little break. Run along and play."

I'm sure Mama won't mind.
After all, Mrs Kiev is just a
harmless
old lady.

It's nice, taking a break from being kind.

I forget all about Benedict until Drumstick kicks the ball over the fence.

The Roost

Escaped Fox!

Wanted (Again)

"You fetch it, Nugget," says Fillet.

"Yeah," says Drumstick.
"You're the smallest."

Not for much longer, I say to myself
as I trudge off to Mrs Kiev's backyard.

Little Scratchings

At first I think Mrs Kiev must have taken
Benedict indoors to keep warm,
because I can't see anyone in the garden.
Then I spot
something
behind the shed.

"Why, Mrs Kiev," I say,
"what are you doing on the barbecue?"

That's strange.
If Mrs Kiev's *here*,
then where's . . . ?

BENEDICT!

That's not Mrs Kiev inside
– it's that mean old fox, Franz.
He's escaped from prison,
nobbled my next-door neighbour
and now . . .

he's going
to EAT
my baby brother!

"CRACK the egg apart," Franz reads aloud,
"and
SCRAMBLE!"

Poor Benedict.
He can hear EVERY word!

I have to help him!

So I creep to the window
and very, very quietly I say,

"Please, Benedict!
I need you to
KICK."

And this time Benedict must
be listening, because . . .

That horrid fox chases right after him,
but I'm taking extra-special care

of my little brother

– and it's my turn

to kick.

WALLOPI

I stay with Benedict until the police arrive.

"I'm sorry," I whisper.
"From now on I promise
to take care of you."

It's not just Benedict
who's listening.
"My little one," says Mama.

She lets me sit on her lap.
The funny thing is
I feel a bit
too big.

It didn't take long for
Benedict to hatch properly.
And guess what?

My name is Nugget
and this is my family.

Florentine

Benedict

↑
Mama

Fillet ↑
& Drumst
(the twi

I'm not the smallest any more . . .

And that's all right with me.